SCOOT

A Tiny New York Bird with a Great Big Idea

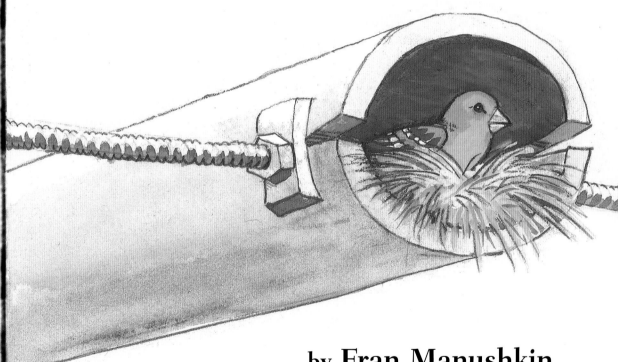

by Fran Manushkin

Illustrated by Bruce Degen

HOLIDAY HOUSE · NEW YORK

Library of Congress Cataloging-in-Publication Data
Names: Manushkin, Fran, author. | Degen, Bruce, illustrator.
Title: Scoot : a Tiny New York Bird with a Great Big Idea / by Fran Manushkin ; illustrated by Bruce Degen.
Description: First edition. | New York : Holiday House, 2022. | Audience: Ages 4–8. | Audience: Grades K–1. | Summary: House
sparrow Scoot is still learning how to manage the busy sidewalks of New York City with the other sparrows, so when she observes
migrating birds struggling with the brilliant city lights, Scoot and her friends help guide them through the confusing skyline.
Identifiers: LCCN 2021040230 | ISBN 9780823442546 (hardcover)
Subjects: LCSH: House sparrow—Juvenile fiction. | Birds—Migration—Juvenile fiction. | Light pollution—Juvenile fiction. | New York
(N.Y.)—Juvenile fiction. | CYAC: House sparrow—Fiction. | Birds—Fiction. | Birds—Migration—Fiction. | Light pollution—Fiction.
New York (N.Y.)—Fiction. | LCGFT: Picture books.
Classification: LCC PZ7.M3195 Sc 2022 | DDC 813.54 [Fic]—dc23/eng/20211004
LC record available at https://lccn.loc.gov/202

ISBN: 978-0-8234-4254-6 (hardcover)

Once there was a little sparrow.
Her nest was cozy,
but kind of narrow.
So what did she do?

She flew!
"Cool view!" she sang,
landing on a stop sign.
What did she see?
A splendid skyline.

What did she smell?
A sidewalk buffet.
"Cool place!" she said.
"I think I'll stay."

Oops!
She almost
got smooshed
by a cowboy boot.
"Scoot!"
 yelled the fellow.
"Scoot! Scoot! Scoot!"

She tripped a lady
in a running suit.
"Scoot!" yelled the lady.
"Scoot! Scoot! Scoot!"

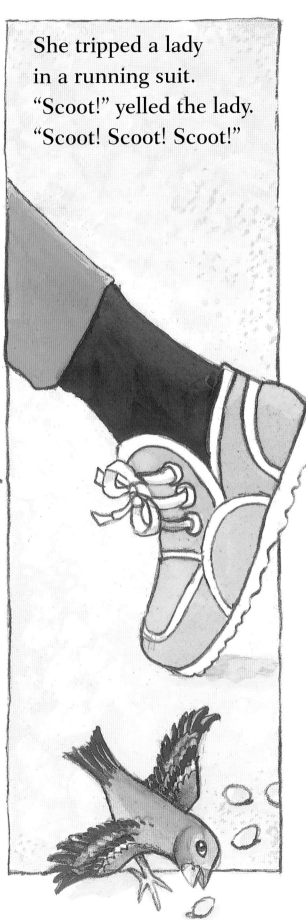

"You need street smarts," chirped an older bird.

"Hop right! Hop left!
Like so, kid:
GO!"

"Okay,"
she told him.
"I'll give it a try."
In two smart hops,
she snatched
a French fry!

"Show me!" sang Scoot.
WHOOSH! Away they flew,
racing the cabs on Fifth Avenue.

In the gutter,
they bumped into Scram's friend *Shoo*.
"Hey, Shoo," said Scram.
"What's up? What's new?"

"Shrimp dumplings," said Shoo, "six juicy grapes,
half a bagel, two chocolate crepes."
Scoot asked, "Is eating *all* you do?"
"What *else* is there?" said Scram and Shoo.

At sundown,
the buildings filled with light.
The bridges wore jewels—
a dreamy sight.
Scram said,
"Let's find a cozy spot,
and rest our feathers
in a parking lot."

Scoot woke up early,
with the rising sun.
The city buzzed
with work to be done!

Scoot saw
shoemakers,   dressmakers,   and bakers,

and filmmakers who
all had important jobs to do.
Scoot wanted one too.

Scoot watched glitzy ladies
singing a song,
shaking a leg
as they danced along.
Scoot tried dancing
on the music hall.
Did anyone watch *her*?
No one at all.

Tour guides told tourists where to go.
Scoot did too. Did they listen?
NO!

The canyons were noisy,
crowded,
and narrow.
"*Scoot!*" yelled everyone,
avoiding the sparrow.

Scoot was small,
but she had heart.
She wanted to help
and do her part.

"Relax! Take it easy.
Have a donut," said Shoo.
"Give up," added Scram.
"What *can* a bird do?"

"We can fly!" said Scoot.
"Follow me! Aim high:
I see a way we can help
in the sky!"

"We *can*?" said Scram,
Shoo,
Vamoose,
and Scurry.

They dropped their donuts
and rose with a flurry.

"Goodbye, cab horns!" said Scoot.
"I can hear my own song."
Hundreds of other birds chirped along:

redstarts,
bluebirds,
warblers—
golden and black-and-white—
chirped and glided,
a colorful sight.

Birds from the southeast
and the southwest
all headed home,
going north to nest.
But their eyes were dazed
by New York's bright night.
Which way *was* north?
Was it left?
Was it right?

"We can help them," said Scoot.
"We have the power.
We can show them the way
from this sky-high tower."
"How can we?" asked Scram,
Vamoose, Scurry, and Shoo.
"Watch me!" said Scoot,
"And do what I do."

Scoot led her flock
in a splendid show,
their kicks pointing north,
past the buildings' glow.
"Have a snack," added Scoot,
"and rest your head.
Central Park is straight ahead."

"Thanks!" sang a bunting.
"What's your name? Who are you?"
"I'm *Sparky*!" Scoot decided.
"*Sparky* through and through."
"I'm *Twinkle!*"
said another.
"I'm *Glitter!*"
"I'm *Glow!*"
"I'm *Star!*"
"From now on,
that's who we are."

"We're cool!" sang Glow.
"We give travelers a lift."
"Who knew," said Glitter,
"that we had a gift?"

Each night,
they greet the birds flying by,
guiding them safely through the bright sky.
At midnight, after a final peep,

five drowsy friends
glide down to sleep.

Five happy friends
snuggling wing to wing.
Even in their dreams—they *sing*!

AUTHOR'S NOTE

New York City is in the middle of a bird migration path called the Atlantic Flyway. Every spring and fall, thousands of birds fly over Manhattan, some of them passing the Empire State Building. Many of these birds stop to rest, feed, and restore their strength in Central Park, called by New York City Audubon "one of the best birding spots in the United States."

Because birds can be confused by the bright lights of skyscrapers, New York City Audubon has created a "Lights Out New York" program, encouraging buildings to turn off their lights at certain hours during spring and fall migrations. The Empire State Building has a policy of turning their lights off at midnight during the heaviest bird traffic. (This is why Scoot and her friends leave the tower at midnight, when their help is no longer needed.)

I wrote the story because I am an avid birdwatcher. I hope my love and enthusiasm for these feisty, fascinating creatures comes through.

For further information, see
http://www.nycaudubon.org/go-birding,
http://www.nycaudubon.org/lights-out-new-york
http://www.audubon.org/conservation/project/lights-out

Fran Manushkin

ILLUSTRATOR'S NOTE

Scoot is a New York tale. I'm a New York bird myself. Born in Brooklyn, New York was my home until my wife, Chris, and I moved to Connecticut some years ago. The sound of New York sparrows having a loud conference in a hedge was the first birdsong I knew.

The New York I wanted to show were places that have memories for me—the observation deck of the Empire State Building and 30 Rockefeller Plaza, the rich decoration of the Chrysler Building, the golden figure on the Municipal Building. I've been in these buildings, visited friends who worked in these buildings, looked out at them from the windows of apartments we lived in.

There are many new buildings in New York, and I am not fond of some of them. I put in the Freedom Tower and the Citicorp Center on Lexington. I remember when Citicorp opened—the big, slanted roofline, the little church tucked under its wing, the stores. We got our son's bedroom furniture from the Conran's Store that was in it.

When Fran wrote about "racing the cabs on Fifth Avenue," I knew I wanted to put in the Library. I was allowed into the collections when I was in graduate school because I was doing research on Albrecht Durer's engravings. The librarians put me in a room and let me hold all these incredible pieces of art. Every time I pass those lions, I go back to that memory.

There are some scenes that are accurate locations, and there are some pages that are collages, so you won't be able to stand on a corner in New York and say, "This is the spot on page X," because this book is not a mapping project. I wanted to show the different realities of New York—how old and how new it is, how vibrant and how quiet it can sometimes be.

Bruce Degen

LANDMARKS INCLUDED IN THIS BOOK

 30 Rockefeller Plaza

 Bethesda Fountain

 Brooklyn Bridge

 Central Park

 Chrysler Building

 Citigroup Center

 Civic Fame Statue

 Consolidated Edison Building

 David N. Dinkins Manhattan Municipal Building

 Empire State Building

 Fifth Avenue

 Helmsley Building

 Metropolitan Life Insurance Tower (commonly known as the MetLife Building)

 One World Trade Center (commonly known as the Freedom Tower)

 Radio City Music Hall

 Stephen A. Schwarzman Building (commonly known as the New York Public Library Main Branch)

 The Plaza

 Washington Square Park

 Woolworth Building

 Zeckendorf Towers